OF SILVER WOLVES AND SONGBIRDS

Short Stories of Tigraen
A novella of Galhadria

Tiffani Sahara

Dusty Rabbit Media, LLC

Of Silver Wolves and Songbirds

Published by Dusty Rabbit Media, LLC.
Denver, CO

Copyright ©2023 by Tiffani Sahara. All rights reserved.

Cover art by Vladimir Kutuzov

No part of this book may be reproduced in any form or by any mechanical means, including information storage and retrieval systems without permission in writing from the publisher/author, except by a reviewer who may quote passages in a review.

FICTION / Fantasy / Collections & Anthologies

Paperback ISBN: 979-8-9889782-2-0

This is a work of fiction. All of the characters, organizations, and events portrayed in this novel are either products of the author's imagination or are used fictitiously.

All rights reserved by Tiffani Sahara and Dusty Rabbit Media, LLC.

Contents

Please read	1
Prequel Stories	
Of Songbirds	7
Of Silver Wolves	23
Deleted Scene	
The First Silver Wolf	45
Alternate View	
A Songbird's Tale:	
Chapter Forty-Nine - Home	53
Thank you	65
More From the World of Galhadria	67
Music from Tigraen	69
About the Author	73

Please Read

A note from the author

Hello dear reader, this small book is for you. Thank you so much for all the love you've shown my characters and my story. I wanted to give you a glimpse of what life was like for Jaren and Songbird before the events of the novel. In addition, exclusive to this print edition you will find a deleted scene as well as an 'alternate' ending and a few illustrations.

Thank you so much for all your support and I look forward to sharing many more stories to come.

Till next time, dear reader. Enjoy!

<3 Tiff

ULTOR

- RSKALAR

THRONGMONGER STRAIT

- RYRROS
- KOLJA
- SORJA
- ARGA-PENTHA
- AIXELL

REVEN WOOD

WHISPERWOODS

TIGRAEN

- BARIZ
- MULK
- DESOL.
- ENX
- ORLORIZ

SHADECRAG MOUNTAINS

- GRAGGAP
- SAUCHVOR

The J

GAZEA

PREQUEL STORIES

These stories take place before the events of "A Songbird's Tale".

OF SONGBIRDS

THE SOUNDS OF THE NIGHT TIME FOREST carried on the cool air. Somewhere in the distance, the low hooting of an owl echoed between the trunks. Pine needles and oak leaves rustled gently in the night. Bats darted between the branches, snapping up moths. Raccoons crept down towards the river to wash their greedy paws.

All alone, on the forest floor, sat a little songbird with a broken wing.

Something moved in the darkness. She pressed herself to the ground, making herself as small as she could. Cloven hooves stirred leaves as they trod towards her. The bird squeezed her eyes shut. Maybe if she was very still and very quiet it would pass her by.

The footsteps sounded like thunder. They stopped right next to her. She heard the shuffling as the creature stopped nearly on top of her. There was a pause.

"What have we here?" Her feathers ruffled as whatever it was began to sniff her. Something warm and rough curled around her and lifted her from the ground. She fluttered helplessly in its hands, her broken wing useless.

"D-d-don't eat me!" She squeaked in terror.

The creature chuckled. "Open thine eyes, look at me."

Songbird slowly opened one eye, then the other. A strange face loomed in front of her, regarding her with green and golden eyes. Glowing orbs hovered in the air around him, bathing the area in soft yellow-orange firefly light.

Of all the fey she had seen in Reven Woods, Ficiun was one of the most unusual-looking. She had always been curious about him, but given him a wide berth, unable to tell if he was friend or foe. He had many of the attributes of a mountain ram, with large spiraling horns and cloven hooves, which were a sharp contrast to the striking Elven shape of his eyes, long arms, and delicate fingers. His skin maintained a bark-like texture from which vines and ivy sprouted at odd intervals.

"Why shouldn't I feast upon thy flesh?"

"B-b-because I wouldn't taste good."

"No?" The rising intonation hinted that he was quite amused. He grinned, flashing sharp bicuspids at her. "If thou would deprive me of a snack, what might thou give me instead?"

"I… I…" She was quaking like a leaf.

"Well?" He reached a long delicate finger towards her, poking her good wing.

Something about his flippant attitude in regards to making her a morsel made her bristle. Songbird puffed up her chest, "You will not eat me! Name your price, but keep your teeth to yourself."

Ficiun threw his head back and laughed. "Well now! I was curious, looking for a brief amusement, but now thou hast garnered my interest. My price is a yarn, so you had best spin me a good one. Prey tell, how thou did break thy wing?"

She tried to settle herself into his palm, but it was like cuddling up with a hungry fox. "It's kind of a long story…"

Songbird perched in the branches, watching the two legs. Over the last few weeks, he had been cutting down trees and slowly assembling some kind of structure in one of the clearings. They didn't get many human visitors in Reven Woods, so his continued presence was especially interesting. She was curious but far too skittish to approach him. All animals knew that two legs were dangerous. Her sister songbirds had told her to stay far, far away from the human. But she'd never seen a human two legs before, so she watched him from afar.

On this particular day, he was using a strange tool to scrape all the bark off several of his logs. His muscles flexed with the repetitive movements under his olive skin. The afternoon sun beat down in the clearing and he was sweating with the effort. He shrugged out of the extra hide he wore. Songbird found herself equally fascinated and mortified by the way the humans could shed or don new hide so easily, even layering multiple hides on. He set his white hide down next to the long red half-hide he normally wore on his back, something silver catching in the light.

Whatever it was looked pretty and she wanted to get a closer look. She waited impatiently, hopping from one foot to another until the human went back to work. Then she darted down to the clearing, landing next to his clothing. The shiny gleam came from a silver cloak pin which was fashioned in the shape of a wolf's head. She tilted her head to the side, examining it carefully. It was as large as she was and looked heavy.

"Hello, little bird. You like my brooch?"

Songbird nearly jumped at the sound of his voice. It was deep and warm and resonant, not at all what she had expected a two-legs to sound like. His tone was friendly, but just to be safe she flew back to the branches.

Silver Wolf Brooch/Cloak Pin by Tiffani Sahara

The human set down his tool and stretched. He ran a hand through his hair, black as raven's feathers, pushing it out of his face. He picked up his back hide, looking fondly at the pin.

"You have good taste, songbird. I think out of everything I've ever done, earning this pin is one of the things I'm most proud of." He smiled wistfully before reaching for his water skin. Uncorking it, he tilted his head back but found it empty. Shrugging, he gathered his skins and headed towards the stream.

Songbird flitted through the trees after the two legs. His steps were light as he went down the trail. Tree roots and rocks jumped out at him, but he moved with the softness and sure-footedness of a wolf. He belonged in the wilds, perfectly at home among the trees. When he reached the stream he dropped his belongings and plunged into the water. He splashed water on his face before filling the water-skin. She could certainly appreciate the joy of a good splash in the water. He wasn't anything like she expected.

Songbird was so focused on watching him that she nearly missed the otterglider swimming across the stream toward the two legs's pile of clothing.

This otterglider was a young one, and his whiskers twitched with excitement as he climbed out of the water and bounded over to the human's belongings. He began to paw through the two legs spare hides. He nosed through everything, his tail twitching excitedly. She hopped along her branch, watching carefully.

"Hey!" She chirped. "What are you doing?"

The otterglider looked up at her and bared his teeth, hissing.

"Hmph. There's no need to be rude." But she hopped a little closer, to keep an eye on him.

The otterglider grabbed the silver brooch in his webbed paws and yanked.

"Don't touch that!" She whistled.

The otterglider bit down on the brooch and pulled. The pin slid free of the fabric and he sprinted off with his prize.

Songbird looked back and forth between the two legs and the fleeing otterglider. She whistled sharply, trying to get the human's attention but he was oblivious. The otterglider scampered up a tree and leaped into the air, spreading the skin between his front and back legs, and gliding gracefully to the next tree. If she didn't go after him now, she would lose him, and then the two legs treasure he had been so proud of would be lost.

"That's not yours!" Songbird flung herself from the branch and spread her wings, flying after him. "That belongs to the two legs."

She wove in and out of the branches as the otterglider scampered up tree trunks and leaped from tree to tree, the silver brooch flashing in its jaws. Tilting her wings, she dove down and gave him a sharp tap on his head with her beak. He hissed through his teeth and turned towards the river, preparing to glide across.

Desperate to catch him before he went into his den she folded her wings tight to her body and sailed after him. He landed on the far bank and Songbird dove straight at him. The little bird landed a sharp blow right to his hindquarters, her beak finding its way through the dense fur to poke his right flank. The otterglider let out a sharp bark, which caused him to drop the brooch. He turned on her, but she flared her wings, flapping and chirping furiously. The young otterglider looked at her, then glanced up into the trees. He chittered angrily but turned and scampered into the forest.

"Hmph." Songbird nodded to herself as she landed next to the brooch. The wolf head grinned at her, glimmering in the sunlight. It held a long, thin, sharp metal needle between its teeth. She tilted her head to the side as she looked at it. *I need to get this back to him. He said it was important.* She tried to clasp it in her beak but it was much too thick to close her beak on, much less lift. Undeterred, she hopped on top of it and tried to grasp it in her tiny talons, but could not get a hold of it quite right. She tried to pinch it in her talons and flapped her wings, but she could not lift it.

"Hmm." She bounced to and fro in the grass, trying to decide what to try next when a conventicle of magpies descended from the trees.

"Magpies? Fie!" Ficiun was holding her in his palm, staring at her intently. He looked ominous in the dim light. His magical firefly orbs cast strange shadows across his face.

"Ye-yes!" Songbird chirped, shivering from the memory. "There were so many of them, and they're much larger than I am."

"Verily, but dear heart, as far as birds go, thou art but a trifle." Ficiun tipped his head, dipping one of his horns to the side as if considering. "Thou were right to stop me from devouring thee. Thy would have made for a most unsatisfying snack."

Songbird shivered again.

Ficiun chuckled. "Prey tell, how didst thou conquer thy magpie foes?"

"Well, well, well… Shalokar's own luck." One of the magpies slunk forward, head down, snapping her beak, eyeing Songbird with dark, beady eyes.

Magpies were just as bad as ottergliders. Songbird sprang to the side, placing herself atop the human's treasure. This, of course, caught the attention of the magpies. They pressed closer, turning their heads to get a look at what she was sitting on.

"What is that?" The lead magpie screeched.

"It's…it's not for you." Songbird chirped.

The magpies shrieked with glee, "A bauble from a human. See how it sparkles? We must have it, we must have it!"

The lead magpie hopped over and pecked at Songbird. "Get away, little bird of song. Relinquish the bauble. I want it for our collection." Songbird winced. It was a warning, but a painful one. The other magpies chortled.

Songbird tried not to tremble. She should just let them have it. What did she care about one mysterious two legs, anyway? But then she thought of him in distress, looking everywhere for his treasure. How proud of it he had been. How would he fasten his long clothing around his shoulders without it? She had never seen him not wear it, even when his other clothing changed.

The first magpie delivered another stab with her beak. This time she meant business. When Songbird did not move the magpie fanned her wings, jumping into the air and pummeling Songbird with her talons, followed by several sharp pecks. Songbird let out a shrill, angry whistle but refused to let go.

She felt a small fire well up inside her little chest. She had chased the otterglider down to recover this herself, and she wasn't going to let the magpies take it from her.

"Go find another treasure, you harpy." Songbird curled her little talons around the edges of the treasure and lay on top of it, defiantly pressing her belly tight against the cold metal.

The magpies shrieked in response. The lead magpie loomed over Songbird, her black feathers glinting blue in the afternoon sun, her dark eyes angry and soulless. She raised her head to deliver another blow when her sister magpies started crowing a great cacophony. Distracted, the magpie turned her head.

Songbird spread her wings and pulled with all her might. The treasure moved, just a little. The magpies were in an uproar and Songbird heaved again, moving the treasure perhaps an inch.

The lead magpie escaped the group, and charged Songbird, buffeting her with her wings. "Enough! Give me the treasure!" She snapped her beak and struck Songbird hard. Songbird let out a shrill whistle as she felt a sharp crack in her right wing.

The magpie lifted her head triumphantly, preparing to strike again. As she was lunging forward a huge pair of fangs clamped onto the magpie.

"Fangs? What monstrous beast now takes the stage in this tale? Was it thy savior or thy ruin?"

Songbird perked up a little. Ficiun seemed genuinely interested in her story. He was sitting on the forest floor, content to continue holding Songbird in his palm. His golden eyes were fixed on her. The leaves stirred in the breeze and the firefly orbs bobbed around playfully, causing the light to dance across the trees. Ficiun nodded, prompting her to continue.

"A bit of both, I suppose. It was a viper."

"A dragon you say?!" The fey teased.

"No, not a dragon, a viper!" Songbird tilted her head, thoughtful. "Although I wonder what it would be like to meet a dragon."

Ficiun scowled, drawing his brows down. "Attune your ears to my wisdom, dragons are best avoided at all costs, do not tangle thy business with their own." He stroked the little bird's head gently with a finger. It was more unsettling than comforting, like a cat toying with a mouse. "Even so, an adder is no mean foe. The fang's kiss brings a poison most potent. Continue."

The viper lunged at the magpie, sinking his fangs into her back. The magpie shrieked as the snake coiled around her. They twisted together on the ground, fighting desperately, while the other magpies clamored in the air above. They might have defended their sister if the viper's strike had not been so sure. Even if the magpie were to escape, she would not have made it, for the venom would have done her in. Songbird was frozen, too scared to move. It seemed the magpies had forgotten her in the chaos of the viper attack.

As the magpies left the bank of the stream, the late afternoon sun cast a golden-orange hue as the final rays pieced the canopy. Last autumn's leaves shifted and crackled softly as a whisper while the dark coils of the adder twisted around its prey. The magpie quivered as the venom did its work. Songbird sat transfixed, utterly horrified as the viper stretched his jaws wide and began to consume the magpie. One little bit at a time, he swallowed the bird alive. It was an eternity before the snake had finished its meal. When he was done, he curled up amongst the leaves, his night and rust-colored scales blending with the foliage. He blinked sleepy eyes as his lazy tongue flicked in and out.

For several long minutes, everything was still. Songbird could only hear the thundering of her blood in her ears. The viper lay just a few feet away, eyes half closed, barely discernible amidst the litterfall.

Maybe if I just sit still, it will leave, Songbird thought. She tried to slow her breathing, but her heart was pounding. The snake had just eaten, surely it couldn't still be hungry. Her wing hung limp at her side. She tried to tuck it close to her body, but it would not move right, and the pain brought black spots into her vision.

Calm down. Think. You're smart, you can figure this out, she told herself. She closed her eyes and took a slow breath. A gentle breeze moved through the forest, tickling her feathers as it passed. Leaves in the canopy rustled softly. Songbird sat as still as possible. The wind had been to her back. The viper's forked tongue came out, languidly tasting the air. At first, nothing. Then, his eyes snapped open.

"I ssssmell desssert." The viper hissed. He slowly drew his coils under him, preparing to strike.

He won't care about the treasure, she thought. *If I can just get away long enough for him to leave, I can come back for it.*

The viper struck. She barely moved in time, making a desperate hop to the side, her lame wing dragging pitifully as she flapped wildly with her good wing. The snake reared up. Stuck between its jaws was the human's treasure. He struggled with it, shaking his head back and forth violently, trying to dislodge it from his mouth. The heavy brooch was lodged behind his fangs. Songbird watched, horrified, as he was unable to spit it out, the viper was forced to swallow it.

Songbird's heart sank as she watched the lump travel down his throat.

"Ah, I sense the closing curtain will be drawing soon upon your tale."

"Yes." Songbird sighed heavily. "The commotion had awakened a great owl and just as the snake was about to try to eat me again, the owl swooped down, grabbed him, and carried him off."

Ficiun stared at her. "And…? That cannot be the ending of thy tale."

"That's all there is."

"I am most unsatisfied with this ending. Sooth, little bird, I am impressed by thy tale. Though this conclusion has come unwelcome anon. "

Songbird pressed herself down into his palm, making herself small under the weight of his displeasure. "I was heading after the owl when you found me." She chirped meekly.

"Truly?" Ficiun looked back the way that they had come, away from the steam and into the woods. "Didst thou hop all that way trying to follow the owl?"

Songbird nodded, her little head bobbing in ascent.

"And didst thou have a plan? How didst thy intend to face the great owl and reclaim thy human's treasure, alone and injured and in the dark?"

"Of course, I have a plan." Songbird whistled defiantly. She absolutely did not have a plan.

"Prey tell, what is it?"

She puffed up her little chest. "Take me to the owl and you'll find out."

Ficiun's eyebrows went up, his golden-green eyes glittering in the firefly light. "Oh, ho, ho! Well now. What a change of character. We learn our dear little trifle is more than she seems." He tapped his chin thoughtfully. "As I am unsatisfied with the conclusion of thy tale as it stands, and I find myself rather in need of an ending, I would be of some assistance. I will aid in the completion of thy adventure. Thou wert so close in attaining thy aim. But first, if thou art to retrieve thy treasure from the deadly bird of night, we must mend thine wing."

The fey suddenly brought his other hand over the top of her, cupping her between his fingers. Songbird whistled in alarm. The fey brought her close to his face and breathed gently into his hands. She could smell pine resin, warm summer grasses, and sharp ivy in his breath. Suddenly his palms were filled with flower petals, pressing softly into her feathers. The mellow aroma of lavender and buttercups soothed the aching in her small body. She could hear Ficiun chanting in the sing-song tongue of the fey distantly.

Just as she was about to fall asleep Ficiun opened his hands and blew on her again. The flower petals scattered and he threw her into the air. Jolted awake by the sudden movement she spread her wings, flapping furiously. She sang out happily as her wings held her aloft. She zipped along the river bank, refreshed and energized, dancing through the petals that were slowly drifting to the ground in the firefly light, her wing along with any aches and pains cured by Ficiun's magic.

"Good now! Let us away anon, and find the bird of night who carried away thy viper."

Songbird swallowed nervously. She perched on one of Ficiun's horns as the fey made his way through the dark forest. The glowing orbs led the way. Branches respectfully parted for Ficiun as he passed, stones and roots seemed to vanish into the ground before his hooves, making the path easy. This was the time that little songbirds should be snuggled safely in their nests. Not out hunting owls with a mercurial fey.

But here she was, trembling with fear and excitement. Trying desperately to come up with a plan.

Ficiun paused before a large, twisting oak tree. There, on a low branch, sat a very large owl. Her eyes were closed, but her ear tufts were upright. In her massive, dark talons was the body of the snake. Blood dripped down from where her nails pieced his scaled hide, making an occasional 'plip' as the drops hit the forest floor. Ficiun tilted his head and reached up to collect Songbird from his right horn. She pressed herself into his palm, quivering.

"Go on." Ficiun drew himself up and reached up towards the branch where the owl was perched. His encouragement was a little *too* eager, apparently finding great amusement in the situation.

"He- hello," Songbird managed. The owl made no move to acknowledge her. She looked back at Ficiun. He was staring at her unnervingly. She cleared her throat and tried again, much louder. "Hello Lady Owl."

The owl opened one orange eye and fixed it on Songbird. She steeled herself. Ficiun was waiting for her to fail, to either flee in fear or to be eaten. Well, she was determined neither would happen. By Shalokar's own teeth, she would retrieve the treasure for the two legs, and she would show Ficiun she wasn't just a hapless morsel of a bird.

"I wanted to say thank you for saving me earlier. You were very gallant, swooping down and snatching the viper before he could eat me. You saved me. And for that I thank you." Her voice quivered at first, but as she spoke she felt herself steady.

Ficiun chortled below. "This was thy plan? To be *polite*?"

Songbird ignored him, but the owl opened her other eye and now stared at Songbird with two great orange orbs that seemed to rival Great Uhel itself in size. Songbird fluttered up from Ficiun's palm, hanging in the air before the owl.

"Please, my lady, if you would be willing to help me one more time? The viper ate something that belongs to... well a friend of mine and I'm trying to return it to him."

The owl tightened her talons, causing the branch to groan. "Oh?" Her low hoot carried through the cool night air.

"Great Lady Owl, I will sing while you sup, and after you're done with your meal, I will collect the treasure and be on my way and I won't trouble you again."

"Does the treasure belong to him?" The owl's eyes moved to Ficiun. He grinned at her in response, flashing sharp bicuspids, still snickering.

"No, lady. It belongs to a two-legs who is making his home here."

There was a long silence. Songbird glanced from the owl to Ficiun, but neither gave any indication as to what they were thinking. The owl seemed to be considering, and blinked her eyes, one first then the other. Ficiun had finally settled into sporting a bemused smirk. His golden firefly orbs bobbed about the tree, casting soft, warm light amidst the branches.

The owl rustled her feathers. "Good. It was brave of you to come to offer thanks, and right that should respect your betters. You have lovely manners for such a small songbird. I will hear you sing and allow you to take your treasure, for I have no need of such things." Said the owl. "And neither does he." She looked pointedly at Ficiun before bending down and tearing into the snake with her sharp beak. Songbird flitted about the gnarled ancient oak, singing. Her sweet serenade filled the glade as the owl ripped long strips of meat from the snake, swallowing them whole. When the owl finally tore into the belly of the snake, something fell to the ground with a heavy thud, catching the moonlight as it tumbled through the air.

Songbird forced herself to be patient and continued her songs until the owl was finished. Then, soft as starlight, she fluttered to the ground. She hopped around the treasure, inspecting it carefully. It was now grimy, but the polished metal shone through here and there. The snarling wolf's head was unmistakable. It was indeed the two-legs's treasure. She jumped onto it, grasping it with her tiny talons, and flapped madly, trying to lift it. The treasure did not budge.

Ficiun laughed heartily as he leaned down and scooped

both Songbird and Jaren's treasure into his hands. "That was most unexpected. What mighty stroke of luck you've had this day, surely you're in Shalokar's favor. Allow me then, if you will, to assist with the conclusion of thy adventure."

The next morning Songbird sat in the branches waiting.

Ficiun had carried her and the trinket all the way back to the two legs's clearing last night. She had flitted back and forth between his thorns the entire way. "Did you see me? Did you hear how sweetly I sang? That was so wonderful, who knew owls were so polite? Do you think I'll get to have another adventure anytime soon?"

After Ficiun set the trinket down on the stump where he was cutting logs the day before, Songbird had declared she would stand guard over it all night to make sure nothing else happened to it. The fey chuckled, his laughter like wind in the grass. He stroked her feathers with the back of a finger. "I'm sure adventure will find you again sooner than you'd like. Until then mine sweet little songbird, I swear on the very heart of Reven Woods that neither harm nor mischief will come to thy human's treasure this night. Rest easy."

She had slept nestled in a pine bough, waking before the sun.

This morning, she sang the sunrise a song of the gallant owl lady who slew the vile viper and saved a brave little songbird.

Now she was perched on the edge of the clearing where the two legs, the human, Ficiun had called him, was building his cabin. She hopped up and down the branch, dancing from one foot to the other with excitement.

At last, he came into the clearing. Today he was accompanied by a female, carrying a bow slung over her shoulder. "Feyn wanted to study today, he's working on some new spell. I swear, your brother spends more time with his nose in a book than anyone I know."

"He's always been like that Wrin." He pushed his dark raven

hair out of his face with one hand, ax slung over his shoulder.

His trinket caught the morning sun, the shimmer drawing his attention immediately. He rushed over to the stump, dropping his ax and scooping up the wolf's head brooch.

"What is it Jaren?" The female asked.

"Thank the Powers, I thought I had lost this." He rubbed it clean on the hem of his cloak and then fastened it into place before turning to face the female. "My pin! I wasn't looking forward to trying to explain to the Interrogers how I had lost mine, But here it was all along…" He paused, sensing he was being watched. But when he looked around the clearing, he saw no one. There was only the sweet melody of birdsong.

Songbird by Tiffani Sahara

OF SILVER WOLVES

"Let me tell you exactly what happened." Feyn steepled his fingers diplomatically as he spoke, looking around the tavern. There were several maidens in here who were excellent prospects for his brother. If he could just catch their attention…

Feyn grinned at his older brother. Jaren sat at the far end of the table, shaking his head. The two of them were just over a year apart and looked nearly identical. Because of this, Feyn kept his face clean-shaven, while Jaren sported a well-trimmed beard. Feyn wore his hair long, in a tail, but Jaren's barely hung to his shoulders. Jaren was every bit a warrior, tall, broad-shouldered, with rippling muscles. Feyn, by comparison, had the body of a scholar who often got so wrapped up in his studies that he forgot to eat, and wielded magic instead of a sword.

Jaren was still wearing his new armor. Feyn had gifted it to him just last year, exquisitely crafted from the finest leather. Feyn had to drag Jaren all the way to Arga-Pentha to be fitted for it. The artisan Feyn had commissioned was said to have made armor for the Tyrant himself, and the Red Shields. The wolf on Jaren's breastplate glistened where it had been recently oiled.

If Feyn could just get his brother to find a woman, maybe then he'd settle down a bit, find some more joy in his life. It'd be good for him. It'd be good for all of them. One of the tavern's serving girls arrived and handed him a pint of beer.

"I'm telling you," Feyn continued loudly, "we would all have been utterly doomed if it wasn't for my brother. We're all safe and able to celebrate because of Jaren."

The serving girl continued to hand pints around the table. "Doomed?" She squeaked.

Wrinnit rolled her eyes. Feyn shrugged at his wife. Wrinnit had grown up with the brothers in Mulk. The three of them played at adventuring as children. Killing rats in the cellar for Pa Tibus, or tracking down lost sheep and cows for the farmers. Now they roamed Tigraen, slaying monsters and helping people where they could.

"Absolutely. You know how dangerous The Pale is. We never would have been able to kill the foul beast if it wasn't for Jaren!" Feyn had caught the attention of the patrons at the near-by tables. The serving girls were starting to take notice. Good.

"Gather round, good folks. Let me tell you a tale."

"This is going to be good." Alceas elbowed Jaren, grinning.

Jaren pinched the bridge of his nose and sighed.

Feyn and Jaren by Flandivel

Jaren knelt, resting his hand on the hilt of his sword. The mud was still soft, the tracks were fresh and made by no beast known to him. He laid his hand in the paw print, his palm barely taking up a third of the indention. The scent of ozone stung his nose, as faint wisps of arcane vapor rose from the prints. Whatever made these had certainly come from The Pale.

Jaren shuddered. He hated magic. The Pale was, perhaps, one of the best examples of why. Over five hundred years ago Ozreus the usurper and his helltouched army had waged war across Tigraen before marching on Sarmatti. The Sarmattians, their army heavily supplemented with exalts, pushed back. Jaren did not know if the Lyn-Tyrians and Gorothkans themselves had been involved, but the sheer devastation that followed had strained the very fabric of reality. Even now, five hundred years later, this no man's land on the border between the two countries was a wasteland where arcane and divine magics ravaged the landscape.

Any battle was hard on a landscape, but a battle of swords could not destroy an area of thousands of square miles the same way the magic had permanently destroyed the area now known as The Pale. The entire region was completely uninhabitable and would be for the rest of eternity as far as anyone knew. No one should wield that kind of destructive power in Jaren's opinion.

When the weather cooperated, you could see The Pale Tower in the distance, perched on a mountain, proudly overlooking the surrounding wasteland that was its namesake. But now, it was a dark winter's night in The Pale. It might stay that way for minutes or years. You never knew. The number of people who strayed into The Pale and made it out again was very, very small. Both Tigraen and Sarmatti patrolled their respective sides of The Pale continuously. Warding stones had been set and meticulously maintained over the centuries. It was one of the few things the countries could cooperate on without dispute. Despite careful attentiveness and constant patrols… *things* still wandered out of The Pale from time to time.

"Mmm." Wrinnit made a sound as she looked over his shoulder, performing her own assessment of the tracks.

Looking back along the trail in the direction the monster had come from, he could see a large warding stone. Faint blue-green light emanated from the carvings in the boulder, barely discernible in the bright summer daylight. About ten paces beyond the warding stone it was the dead of night, the grass was blanketed in thick snow. Pearlescent mist swirled in the dark, obscuring his view. The Pale was like that. Summer day outside, winter night inside; the time of day or the weather could change in an instant and without warning.

Shaking his head, Jaren stood. "Stay alert. I'm not sure what we're dealing with, but it will be large and incredibly dangerous."

Feyn leaned on his staff. "You don't have to tell us."

"At least there's only one." Alceas shrugged, ever the optimist.

"That we know of." Jaren cautioned.

The pack turned away from The Pale and followed the tracks. Wrinnit took the lead with Jaren immediately behind. Feyn and Alceas brought up the rear. The tracks led them to a small camp, which had been ravaged. The fire had been out for some time, the stones containing the coals scattered. Deep gouges in the earth were present where the beast had clawed the ground. Blankets were strewn about. Packs had been torn open, camping supplies littered the area. Deep rust-colored splotches stained the grass.

Spreading out, the pack drew their weapons. Jaren held his sword at the ready, eyes scanning the area. Nothing but grasslands in any direction. The men positioned themselves around the edge of the camp while Wrinnit examined the carnage.

The grass waved gently in the slight breeze. Insects buzzed in the late morning sun. Meadowlarks sang out from among the stalks. Jaren kept his breathing slow and steady, inhaling through his nose.

"Most likely a patrol camp. Four scouts. At least two of them didn't make it." Wrinnit finally announced. "Whatever came out of The Pale tore through here like a demon. Survivors ran east." She gestured.

"And the beast?" Jaren asked.

Wrinnit nocked an arrow on her bowstring, eyeing the eastern horizon. "That's where things get a little tricky. The tracks just sort of… disappear."

Feyn was interrupted by the gasp of a woman near the end of the table. A pretty serving girl was hovering close to the table, it was her gasp that had given pause. She was pretty, buxom with soft features and long blonde hair. She held her pitcher of ale close to her chest.

Jaren, Alceas, Wrinnit, and Feyn were sitting at a large table. They had already been joined by three others. Patrons from other tables close by had angled themselves better to hear the story from their own seats.

"My lady, perhaps you should sit. Our story becomes much more distressing. I would hate for you to faint." Feyn patted a small gap on the bench next to Jaren. She sat obediently, stealing a shy glance at Jaren, and blushing in response when he looked at her.

Feyn tried not to smile. Irritation was painted all over his older brother's face. *Well, too bad*, he thought. *If you're too stubborn to go get yourself a woman, I'll find a way to bring them to you.*

"Go on then, tell them what happened next Feyn." Alceas encouraged from his spot on the other side of Jaren.

Jaren and Wrinnit exchanged places and he walked slowly through the camp, observing the damage.

"We should follow the survivor's tracks. They're likely in need of help, and their situation may be dire." Alceas urged.

Feyn nodded in agreement. "If we can find them, we may be able to get more information on what they faced."

There were two sets of tracks leading away from the camp. One pair belonged to someone wearing boots, likely male, based on the size and shape of the footprints. The other tracks portrayed bare feet. These didn't make much sense. They were smaller, and humanoid, but the cadence was off. He could see whoever had run had struggled in their flight. Either they were injured, or very weak. They had fallen several times, and their footprints were muddled as if they had drug their feet. The massive, monstrous tracks from the border were nowhere to be seen.

"Alright," Jaren agreed, his eyes following the path the patrol had fled. "Let's go find them."

The pack didn't have to walk long before Wrinnit held up her hand, stopping the group. Jaren held his breath, listening carefully. There, past the buzzing insects and the meadowlarks singing, was quiet sobbing. He and Wrinnit made eye contact and she gave him a single nod before turning her head to the right and nodding in that direction. Jaren gave her a nod back, bringing his sword to the ready.

She waited for him to signal Feyn and Alceas before stepping forward into the tall grass.

"Come out." She ordered. "We can hear you. We're here to help."

When there was no response Jaren waded past her into the grass. Feyn and Alceas kept a watchful eye, always wary of traps, while Wrinnit moved off to the side, bow at the ready.

Huddled amidst the tall stalks of prairie grass, was the most frail old man Jaren had ever seen. He was gaunt, his arms and legs rail thin. A tattered loincloth clung to his bony hips. He was shaking and sobbing.

"Alceas, bring a cloak."

Alceas tromped through the grass, his heavy plate mail clanking. "Oh. Mersey have mercy." He knelt, wrapping a heavy wool cloak around the shivering old man. "What's your name?"

"Name? Name? Name?" The man repeated between sobs and hiccups.

Jaren and Alceas exchanged a glance.

"You're alright man, take a breath." Alceas said gently.

"Breath, breath, breath, breath." The man repeated, though this time with less hysteria.

"That's a good man. Can you tell us anything?"

"Anything? Anything?"

Alceas looked back up at Jaren. "I can try a prayer?"

"Prayer! Prayer!" The senior crowed. He was calming down quite a bit at this point, but seemed unable to form his own thoughts or sentences.

"If you think that's best. He may be in shock," Jaren hesitated, "Though it is a little strange to have such an old one so far from town. What would he be doing out here alone? Can he even walk? He must be pushing ninety winters by the look of him."

Feyn had wandered over to see what hold up was. "Holy Skylae! You're not kidding."

"Maybe he wandered into The Pale?" Alceas mused.

The old man began to rock slightly, hugging the cloak tight to him, muttering the last words of each of their sentences.

Jaren frowned. Did the man's face look a little less gaunt? "All the more reason to be extra cautious."

"Cautious, cautious, cautious." The elder's words faded to

whispers.

Feyn rolled his eyes. "You are suspicious of everything."

"You're welcome for keeping you alive." Jaren shot back.

"I'm going to pray over him." Alceas placed a firm hand on the man's shoulder.

Alceas began to pray, his strong voice petitioning Skylae for aid. His voice carried, loud against the low hum of the ambient prairie sounds. The elderly man repeated the words of the invocation. The louder Alceas spoke, the louder the man repeated his words. Encouraged, Alceas continued his prayer.

Jaren maintained his grip on the hilt of his blade, unable to shake the feeling that something was off. He squinted. It wasn't just his imagination. The man's face began to fill out, his wrinkles receding. His near skeletal hands began to swell as they clung to the dark wool cloak. Jaren had seen Alceas's prayers work many times, and this was not how divine healing happened.

Out of the corner of his eye he saw Wrinnit snap her attention to something, drawing her bow. A ragged young man was running towards them, wearing a patrol cloak, shouting. "STOP! STOP RIGHT NOW, GET AWAY FROM HIM!"

There was a sharp crack and black smoke burst into the air.

"Crack!" Feyn shouted, slamming his hands down on the table theatrically.

The young woman seated next to Jaren jumped, nearly spilling the contents of the pitcher she still clung to. Jaren gently took it from her and set it on the table. She blushed as their fingers brushed before looking back at Feyn, eager for him to continue.

"Then what happened?" She ventured.

There was quite a crowd gathered around by now. Other women had started to cluster towards the far end of the table, near Jaren and Alceas.

"Oh, Powers. I see my story has interrupted everyone's fine evening. I do beg your sincere forgiveness." Feyn did his best to sound apologetic.

"You know damn well your business, man. And you've done a good job of it too. Get on with the telling, wizard." A large fiery bearded man from the next table shouted.

Feyn bowed. "Of course, good sir."

Jaren barely brought his sword up in time to block. Looming over him was a creature, blacker than ink, shrouded in swirling smoke. It was hard to get a sense of its shape, but it had a head reminiscent of a canine, and massive limbs disjointed, ending in large humanoid paws with wicked claws. *There you are*, Jaren thought. *Here is the beast that made the tracks.*

One of its paws gripped Jaren's sword while it struggled to pin Alceas down with the other, the metal of his armor groaning under the weight.

"Scit!" Feyn was stumbling backward, putting as much distance between himself and the monster as he could.

A dozen canine-esque heads emerged from the smoke. "Scit! Scit! Scit!" Each of the heads imitated, mocking. Each mouth was overfilled with razor-sharp teeth. There seemed to be no discernible eyes.

An arrow zipped through the air and embedded itself into what might have passed for the main head. The monster winced but made no sound.

Jaren lunged to the side, away from Alceas, relying on the

Vendarian style for his parry and counter. As he hoped it would, the creature followed him, shifting its weight, and allowing Alceas to roll away and climb to his feet.

The man who had tried to warn them was screaming again.

"Shut up, fool!" Jaren could barely make out Wrinnit's voice above the man's hollering. She was yelling at him. "You'll draw its attention."

But the patrolman was already charging forward, sword drawn. "By the Powers, I'll kill you!"

As he drew closer Jaren could see he was young, perhaps not even twenty winters. *Moons Above.*

The creature was still growing in size, each of its many mouths screaming back at the young man. "Kill you, kill you, kill you!" It mocked.

Jaren whipped his blade around and made for the creature, trying to keep its attention focused on him while Alceas came in to flank the beast and Feyn prepared a spell. Jaren had never seen a beast like this before, but he sensed they needed to end it before the thing became too large to handle.

Alceas slammed his mace into the creature's leg. There was a crunch as the knee shattered and bent the wrong way. The creature's only reaction was to turn around and slam a paw into Alceas, denting his breastplate and sending him sliding through the grass.

Jaren brought his blade down, slicing through the creature's side. The smoke parted enough to display black and gray mottled flesh that dripped black ichor from where it had been cut. The monster launched itself back at Jaren, unphased by either injury. Jaren dodged, but the young patrolman charged past him, brandishing a sword.

"Die!"

"Die! Die! Die!"

The young man stabbed the sword into the monster, who jerked back, wrenching the sword from his hands. He screamed in frustration and the many mouths of the monster screamed back at him, smoke billowing around them, the beast looming ever larger. It was at least two heads taller than Jaren by now, and growing with the chaos.

Jaren grabbed the young man by the back of his gambeson and yanked him backward, away from the creature right as the monster's paw smashed into the ground where the man stood.

"Stop your screaming." The young man struggled, in a panic. Jaren continued to pull him back from the monster, "Calm down. Get a hold of yourself."

Green arcane light blossomed from the side of the creature where Feyn's spell slammed into it. Another arrow from Wrinnit landed in one of the beast's faces. Alceas fell upon it with his mace. Jaren had pulled the patrolman to a safe distance, keeping his eyes on the fight the entire time. While his pack harried the creature, it made no sound. It appeared agitated, but nothing seemed to injure it or have any effect. Whenever one of his friends called to the other to communicate, it echoed their last words.

That's it!

"Everyone! Back away from it. From here on out, make no sound what-so-ever!" Jaren yelled.

"What-so-ever! Ever! Ever!" The creature's many maws called, their teeth clacking together ominously.

But the pack did as Jaren commanded, everyone withdrew cautiously, weapons raised.

The creature cocked what seemed to be the main head, tilting it like a dog listening for its master's call. The young patrolman took a breath as if to speak. Jaren clamped a hand over his mouth. *Just watch*, Jaren silently urged.

The beast sniffed the ground, black smoke drifting through the tall grass. As it sniffed, it began to shrink. Its movements became more urgent, cocking its head and listening, then moving towards even the slightest of sounds, frantic for some kind of input. Feyn, Wrinnit, and Alceas froze.

Frantic, the thing crawled through the grass, its disjointed legs looking more spider-like as it made its way toward Jaren. The creature was almost upon him, black smoke filling the air. Jaren held his breath and kept his hand tight over the young man's mouth. The creature continued to shrink, the smoke drawing back inward, until suddenly, there was an old man quivering in the grass before them.

The entire tavern was looking at Feyn. Many patrons appeared to be holding their breath.

"Feyn, you don't—" Jaren started, breaking the stillness.

"SHHHH!!!" A chorus rose from the tavern, swiftly silencing him.

Feyn gave his brother a half-cocked grin and shrugged apologetically. Jaren half-heartedly waved a an in the air as if to say to his brother, *"Well, go on then. Let's get this over with."*

"And then?" The golden-haired maiden seated next to Jaren asked, eyes wide. She had her hands clasped tightly together, held against her chest.

Jaren exhaled carefully. He let go of the man and motioned for him to stay quiet. The patrolman nodded, his face pale. After sheathing his sword as gingerly as possible, Jaren made his way slowly over to Feyn. As long as there was no noise above the ambient sounds of the insects and the birds, the creature maintained the shape of the old man.

Jaren pantomimed to his brother until at last Feyn nodded and produced the stump of a tallow candle from his pack. Jaren pulled his gloves off and went to work. He took his hunting knife and shredded the edge of his cloak. Then he warmed the tallow in his hands and mixed it with the fabric fibers. When he had two tiny balls of wax and wool fibers in his hands, he went back to the old man.

Kneeling, he reached for the old man. He flinched away. Jaren nodded reassuringly, keeping his movements slow. He held up the wax to show the elder. Gently he pressed the tallow-wool mixture into one ear of the man's ears, then the other.

At first, nothing happened. But then the old man began to weep. He smiled a gap-toothed smile at Jaren, eyes filled with relief. The tallow and the wool completely plugged his ears. He touched Jaren's hands in thanks before his eyes rolled up into his head and he leaned precariously to the side. Jaren eased him down. The elder lay his head in the grass and died.

Silence.

"And thus, my brother solved the riddle of the echo-beast and saved the youngest ranger to patrol The Pale." Feyn finished with a sweeping bow.

The room erupted into a cacophony of cheering and applause.

The maiden seated at the table turned to Jaren, her eyes wide and luminous. "How did you know?"

Jaren shrugged. "It echoed everything we said. The louder things were the bigger it got. You can't touch or harm an echo, but if you don't make noise, it can't echo back."

"You starved it." She reasoned.

Jaren nodded, "I suppose you could put it that way, yes."

She leaned towards him, twirling a strand of her golden hair through her fingers. "It must get lonely, out on the trail all the time."

"Sometimes," Jaren admitted.

She leaned further in his direction, the swell of her breasts peeking out over the top of her corset. Feyn tried not to stare. The maiden shimmied closer to him on the bench, and leaned over, whispering in Jaren's ear. She moved back, looking up at Jaren through her lashes.

Feyn watched his brother consider it. Jaren kept his expression neutral, hesitating. *Come on,* Feyn urged silently. *She's throwing herself at you, what more do you want?*

Just then, several of the tavern's serving maids came over with pitchers.

"A drink for our hero?"

"It's not every day we get to meet a real silver wolf."

"That was so brave and so clever of you."

The women pressed in around him.

"If you'll please excuse me." Jaren rose from the table. "I think I'm in need of some fresh air." Jaren wove his way through the tavern, doing his best to politely accept claps on the back and firm handshakes as well as thanks from the patrons before finally making his way out the door and into the night.

Feyn shook his head. So close. He hardly noticed when Wrinnit wrapped her arms around him and kissed him on the cheek. "What's wrong, dear?"

"Why is he like that?" Feyn complained. "I do all that work and the women come flocking over, and he flees."

"You know how much Jaren hates being the center of attention." Wrinnit reminded her husband gently. "I know you think your intentions are good, but I don't think that's the best way to encourage your brother to find a woman."

Feyn frowned, staring at the door. "He's got all of us, but I know he's lonely. He needs someone. He needs something like you and I have."

"Maybe he's just not ready. Besides, can you really see your brother falling for a starry-eyed serving woman who would throw herself at him so easily? That's not his preference."

Feyn ran a hand over his face. "I know, I know. But you can't blame me for trying."

Wrinnit kissed Feyn's cheek again and untangled her arms from around him. "Why don't you go talk to him."

Jaren took a long draw on his pipe, exhaling slowly, watching the smoke drift towards the starlit sky. It was a warm summer night, and the land was aglow with the gentle orange light of Great Uhel. He heaved a sigh.

The tavern door opened and Jaren braced himself for the flock of women who were surely coming after him.

"Nice night for a smoke." Feyn offered.

Jaren exhaled, his body immediately relaxing. His brother's company was always welcome. Ever since they had been small, the two of them had been close.

Crickets chirped from the weeds near the side of the building. The aroma of pipe tobacco hung in the air. The two men stood in silence, Jaren leaning up against the tavern wall, smoking his pipe quietly. Feyn stood with his hands on hips, just as he did when he was a lad, examining the stars, searching for constellations.

"Look, Jaren…"

"Don't worry about it, Feyn. I know you enjoy that sort of thing. Some days I wonder why you took up a spell book and not a lute."

"Easier to follow you around with a spell book," Feyn said smoothly.

The door to the tavern opened again and one of the patrons stumbled out and around the corner of the building.

"Wrin and I have been talking. We think a woman would do

you some good."

Jaren puffed at his pipe. The crickets kept chirping. Around the side of the building came a relieved moan of a man who was emptying his bladder against the side of the building.

"What about Sovyn back in Mulk? She had *such* a set of breasts on her." Feyn gestured for emphasis.

"She's married now."

Feyn turned to Jaren, "Oh? Is she?"

"Was last time we were home."

"Hm. Well, what about Faledra? Weren't you interested in her for a while?"

Jaren blew a smoke ring. "She moved to Bariz with her husband two summers ago."

Feyn frowned. He pulled absently at his chin. "Echila?"

Jaren gave Feyn a hard stare.

The younger brother put his hands up. "Now, now, I know she's not much to look at, but she's smart. She'd make a good wife."

The man stumbled back around to the front of the building. He nodded to Feyn and Jaren, throwing open the tavern door. Light and sound flooded into the street as he staggered over the threshold, slamming the door behind him. The street was dark again.

"You got the only good one." Jaren finally said.

"Pardon?"

"You got the only good one," Jaren repeated. "Women who don't mind traveling cross country on foot, who know how to ride a horse, who can stand sleeping on the ground, who know how to hunt for their own food, who are willing to risk their lives to kill monsters... they're damn hard to find. And they're certainly not serving ale in taverns."

"Well you could at least have some fun while we try to track down this legendary woman of your dreams."

Jaren scowled. "I wouldn't disgrace a woman by sleeping with her if I don't have any intention of—"

"Powers, Jaren. I'm not saying you have to bed the woman. But would it kill you to enjoy her company? Compliment a woman, let her compliment you. There's no harm in flirting. I'm sure Mersey would forgive you for sharing a chaste kiss. My point is, how will you know if you've found your one if you won't even talk to the woman?" Feyn had crossed his arms and was standing stiffly. "Is it so wrong for a man to want his brother to be happy?"

"Alright. Alright." Jaren reluctantly tapped out his pipe.

"Just try to enjoy the attention for once, eh?" Feyn opened the door to the tavern and bowed, gesturing for his brother to enter ahead of him.

Jaren sighed. Warmth and golden light, the smell of ale and cooking meat and hot bread bathed him as he headed into the Tavern. There, seated at the table next to Wrinnit and Alceas, the golden-haired, doe-eyed girl was waiting for him.

DELETED SCENE

A SCENE THAT DID NOT MAKE THE FINAL CUT OF THE NOVEL "A SONGBIRD'S TALE".

On the road between Aixell and the Whisperwoods

The First Silver Wolf

One night Songbird lay wrapped in her blanket, drowsy, but unable to drift off. She was watching Jaren from across the fire. He was sitting opposite her, carefully oiling his blade by the firelight. The coals were burning low, casting flickering shadows across the handsome angles of his face.

"Jaren?" She ventured. He fixed his eyes on her, deep green like pine boughs in shadow, and she felt her heart beat a little faster under his gaze. "Who taught you how to fight?"

Jaren returned to oiling his blade. "When I was a boy, I trained with the garrison in Mulk, under the direction of Sir Hardric. When I was older, I became a soldier and served with the other men-at-arms in Sir Hardric's service."

She rolled onto her side so she could face him better. "What's a garrison?"

"A group of soldiers who are stationed in a location to protect it." Jaren held his sword out and looked down the length of the blade, inspecting it, turning it in the limited firelight.

"Who is Sir Hardric? How did he learn how to fight?"

"Sir Hardric is a Black Bull, he's the knight who governs Mulk. He was probably trained by his father, or another knight. And before you ask," Jaren teased, "a knight is someone who is considered nobility, which means they hold land and title. Common folk pay tribute to him and in return he protects and governs them." Jaren sheathed his sword.

As Jaren was being particularly agreeable, she had no choice but to ask more questions. "If Sir Hardric was a Black Bull, when you served him in the garrison, er, man-at-arms, was that what made you a Silver Wolf?"

Jaren had turned to straightening his bedroll as he answered, "No. Sir Hardric and I had... A disagreement. We parted ways and I decided to fight on my own. In Tigraen, when you fight in an organized group under nobility in service to your country, you're a man-at-arms, a soldier. If you fight for anyone who will pay you, you're a mercenary. If you choose to fight for the people and the land of your own accord... We refer to those people as Silver Wolves."

She propped herself up on her elbow. "Why do you call them Silver Wolves?"

He heaved a sigh and, relenting, tossed another log on the coals. Sparks danced the air, like small fireflies against the black night sky. Jaren rose and went to the saddle bags. If he was going to tell this tale, he may as well smoke a pipe.

"The land of Tigraen has been beset by infernal powers since the time of Ozreus." He told her as he unpacked his pipe and his tobacco. "Why the Gorothkans first began to covet the land, who can say; although since they started they've never relented. But Tigraen is strong, and neither the land nor her people will suffer the yoke of evil. It is said that even the birds of the air and the beasts of the forest will rise to her defense and protect Tigraen from the Enemy."

A mixture of pride and wonder filled Songbird. She was coming to Tigraen's aid in its time of need. Had there been others before her? Small flames licked up the edges of the log until it finally caught. The fire leapt up, blazing, fighting back the shadows of night. Songbird was wide awake now and sat up, attentive, pulling her knees to her chest and wrapping her arms around her legs.

"There is an old tale…" Jaren continued, his voice low and steady, as he packed his pipe, "about a warrior from the north, Morven of Ryrros. A skilled fighter and hunter, Morven was blessed with many children, and though he had lost his wife in childbearing, their family was happy. They lived on a small farm, far from any town, and made their way peacefully for many years. But as is the way of things, their peace was not meant to last forever."

The coals popped ominously, sending sparks into the air. Jaren lit his pipe, puffing to get the tobacco burning. Songbird shifted, pulling her blanket around her shoulders.

"One year, winter came early. The snows blew cold and hard off the Throngmonger straights for weeks and weeks on end. In the depths of winter, food was particularly scarce and Morven had to range farther than normal to find game. Of his children, his eldest was a daughter, fair and strong with beautiful long dark hair, and she frequently took care of her younger brothers and sister when their father went hunting.

Morven ranged far, tracking a strong buck through the deep snow. At last he came across the buck in a quiet clearing. He drew his arrow, aiming carefully. He was about to loose the arrow when the howling of wolves echoed through the woods, startling the buck, who sprinted away. After the buck had gone, a great white wolf crossed the clearing, pausing to look at the warrior, before moving on."

Jaren took a draw on the pipe, the scent of the tobacco smoke mixed with the campfire smoke. "Morven tracked the buck further into the woods, determined not to lose his chance to feed his family. He felt the wolf watching him from the trees, as if the two were tracking in tandem. When he found the buck a second time, the wolf prowled out from the trees, startling the buck into flight again. Morven turned his bow towards the wolf, but the wolf leapt easily away, and disappeared into the forest. A chorus of howls filled the air a second time."

Songbird looked at the dark lands around them, listening. She had been familiar with all the wolves in Reven woods, but had yet to encounter one as a woman.

"Morven, frustrated and determined, pressed on, following the buck's tracks. He had not gotten far, when the great wolf stepped out from the trees and stood in his path. Morven drew his bow, but the wolf regarded him without fear. Five wolf cubs wandered out from the trees to stand behind the wolf. It gave Morven pause. Why would a wolf cub be born out of season? It was then Morven understood that it was an omen. He immediately shouldered his bow and hurried towards home."

"How did he know it was an omen? What kind of omen? What does that mean?" Songbird chirped.

Jaren quirked an eyebrow at her as he took a draw on his pipe, "Did you want to hear the end of the story or not?"

She frowned, slumping down, squeezing her legs back to her chest, but remained quiet.

"Morven raced home. Trekking through the deep snow was exhausting, and night was well on its way, but he would not give up. Unfortunately, by the time he arrived, it was too late. His home had been ransacked, and his eldest daughter had been slain, her body lay in the red snow where she had fallen. Morven wept with grief, and in his sorrow he nearly missed the small cries of his younger children.

"His eldest had given her life so her younger siblings could escape and find cover in the woods. The children found their father and told him how they had fled from a group of trolls raiding from across the Throngmonger straights, how their sister had stayed behind to cover their escape, and how a great white wolf had appeared and hid them safely in the forest.

"The wolf appeared to Morven again, its white fur glistening like pure silver in the moonlight. The wolf nodded to Morven, before going over to his daughter's body. The white wolf breathed on her, and her body vanished, turned to mist or snow by ancient magics. In its place, a she-wolf now stood, fair and strong, with beautiful dark fur. The white wolf led the she-wolf off into the night.

"He vowed, then, to do everything in his power to prevent any more daughters of Tigraen from falling unnecessarily. Morven and his remaining children became the first Silver Wolves of Tigraen, traveling around, fighting monsters, and doing what good they could for the common people living in the remote and wild places of Tigraen."

Songbird felt a little sad. "Why did the wolf take the daughter away?"

"Daughters of Tigraen are not soft and sentimental as our Sarmatti cousins. Our women are fighters till the end, and so she returned to the land that bore her to continue defending Tigraen." Jaren's tone was somber, but there was a familiar intensity there, burning just below the surface.

A lone cricket chirped near the edge of camp. The log had burned down to coals and the light from the fire had died down to softly flickering light. Songbird looked at Jaren, the proud angles of his face, and his dark hair. His eyes met hers from across the fire. She lay down, rolled over and put her back to the fire, trying to ignore the rapid beating of her heart.

Alternate View

The ending scene from the other character's perspective.

Major spoilers for "A Songbird's Tale".

Chapter Forty-Nine
Home

Songbird had been looking for Ficiun for weeks. The fey had made himself scare. Songbird combed the woods, flitting from one tree to the next, looking in all the places she knew him to frequent. Ficiun was determined not be found. Still, she did not give up.

A fear had settled over her like a wet cloak. She worried that if she did not find Ficiun before the snows fell that she might forget what it was to be a woman. Songbird did not want to forget. She wanted Jaren. As her desperation grew, she ranged further and further from the cabin.

At last, having ranged to the very northernmost edge of Reven wood, she found him. Ficiun was sitting in a clearing, watching the leaves fall. She flew to him and landed in font of him, chirping as loudly as she could to get his attention. "I have been looking everywhere for you."

"Oh weary morsel, what dost thou want?"

Ficiun's eyes were distant, his tone somber.

"I beg your pardon!" Songbird puffed her chest and launched herself into the air, flitting about his head. "Is that really how you're going to address me? I'm not a *just* a little bird, much less a weary morsel. I am Songbird, the Spider Slayer, the Scourge of the Manticore, and the Ruin of Arzinock, and I need to talk to you."

Ficiun tilted his head and quirked an eyebrow inquisitively. He held out a hand and she landed in his palm, rustling her feathers.

"Now that I have your attention. I came to ask you to change me back, please." She dipped her head down in a movement the was something of a curtsy.

"Thou wert to change back into thy true form should any real danger befall you. Thou art here before me as a bird, which should mean that thou hast failed in thy quest, yet thou sayest that Arzinock was defeated?"

"Yes!" Songbird hopped from one foot to the other impatiently. "Jaren and I killed Arzinock. We completed my quest."

Ficiun rubbed his chin with his free hand. "Little bird of many titles, I felt the spell I had placed upon thee break in a most violent manner."

"Ah. I think that happened when Arzinock squished me," she admitted. "I thought I was going to die. He had me in his claws and I hurt him with my magic so Jaren could attack him and then he slammed me into the ground. I thought for sure I wouldn't make it. Everything went black and when I opened my eyes I was a bird again."

"Verily?"

"If you don't believe me, come and see Jaren."

"How didst thou come by magic of a caliber that would hurt a Gorothkan."

"Tetsu gave it to me. She said you didn't do a good enough job of equipping me, so she helped me."

Ficiun brought Songbird close to his face. He closed his eyes and took a long, slow, inhale through his nostrils. When he opened his eyes, his expression was dark. "Thou met an offspring of the vile and most hated Tiamat. Her mark is upon you."

"Honored daughter." Songbird correct. "Tetsu is an honored daughter of Tiamat. And the princess of Sho."

Ficiun narrowed his eyes at her. "Thou would do well to watch thine tongue in my presence. Thou knowest not of what thy speak. We have no love for Tiamat or her children."

"I'm not afraid of you. After facing Arzinock, you're really not that scary. And Tetsu doesn't like you either, so the feeling is mutual."

"Thou art a child of Shalokar, thou hast no place among her kind." Ficiun hissed.

Songbird lifted her head defiantly. "I can be friends with whoever I want. Now, are you going to change me back or not?"

"I would speak with thy Jaren. Mayhaps he is glad to be rid of thee. Mayhaps he is pleased that thou hast returned to thy true form."

Songbird spread her wings, "I'll take you to him, but prepare to be disappointed."

"Hurry, Ficiun! We're almost there." Songbird was swooping between branches, racing ahead and then doubling back to check on Ficiun's progress. She felt he was moving at a deliberately and unnecessarily slow pace.

"Truly, I had forgotten how exhausting thou art as a traveling companion. Verily, didst Jaren put up with thee all those many months?" Ficiun moved slowly through the forest, tree branches and undergrowth moving out of his path respectfully.

"Jaren loves me." Songbird sang.

Ficiun snorted.

Songbird came to rest on a low branch, waiting for Ficiun to catch up with her. "Why did you want us to go kill Arzinock anyway?"

The sun was streaming through the patchy canopy of oaks and pines. The few leaves that still clung to the ancient oaks were a blaze of deep reds and dark browns, which scratched together in the breeze. The forest fey tilted his head, inviting Songbird to move to one of his long spiraling horns.

"As thou has slain the demon, I will tell thee, as a token of my gratitude. And in hopes that it will cease thine incessant warbling and hassling of mine pace."

Songbird rolled her eyes. *If you wouldn't walk so slowly, I wouldn't have to keep asking you to hurry.*

"Years ago, there was a maiden most fare. She was a perfect vision of loveliness, few mortals can make such a claim. Her skin held the perfect golden hue of a sunset and her hair dark as the night sky. Often, she would come to my forest to pick flowers and to sing, and in time. As delicate and tender and sweet as a wildflower, so was her nature. Sooth, in time I became quite fond of her."

Ficiun had grown quiet, as if he could somehow pluck her from his memory and make her real, if only for a moment. Songbird could feel the sorrow about him like a funeral shroud. She waited patiently for him to continue.

"Her name was Yvette." He finally said with some difficulty. "She was the daughter of a Count and her brainless, witless, vapid father married her off to a harsh, weak-minded imbecile of a man in the south who didn't deserve her. When I could get news of her, I was not surprised to learn that she was able to tame even his blistering nature. And then that damned demon and his accursed cultists murdered her. By the time I caught wind of treachery brewing, it was too late. Jaren and I are kin in that matter, having both lost someone to the Arzyntine. Those vile, wretched, stinking devils took her from me. They put out the light of something most beautiful in the world, something that I treasured dearly, and for that I will never forgive them."

The bird and the fey traveled on in silence.

"Here! He's here!" Songbird burst through the trees into the clearing. "Jaren, I brought him, I brought Ficiun." She sang to him, knowing he could not understand her, but unable to help herself. Her little chest ached at the thought. How she missed talking to him.

Ficiun followed her into the clearing, his cloven hooves crunching on the fall leaves.

"You." Jaren narrowed his eyes, clenching his hands into fists.

Ficiun put one hand on his chest and made an extravagant low bow, dipping his head. "Sooth. It is as you say. I am I."

"Why?" Jaren demanded.

"I am I for this is the shape my Lord Shalokar has fashioned me into. And you are you for your Powers have shaped you thus."

Jaren stepped towards the fey, leaves crackling beneath his boots. "That's not what I meant and you know it, trickster. Why did you pick Songbird, why did you send her out to take on a demon that she had absolutely no hope of defeating? Why send her to her death? Why!?" His voice shook the stillness of the clearing.

Ficiun regarded him coolly, disdain evident in his green and golden eyes. "Jaren, thine inane line of questioning continues to confound mine logic. Mine reasons for hating the demon are mine own. You know very well the answers to your other inquiries. I sent her in your stead because you would not go. Thou questions occurrences which did not happen. Whether or no there was no hope for her success, the pair of you were successful, were you now? Arzinock is no more. Neither is dead, but quick and present with us even now. How can thou say there was no hope and that she was sent to her death when neither of those things came to pass?"

Ficiun held his hand out and Songbird flew to it. "Please be gentle with him," she chirped. "Think of Yvette."

Jaren was trying to keep his composure, but Songbird could

see in the tightness of his jaw and the clench of his fists that he was livid. "Change. Her. Back."

"Ah, but now it is my turn to inquire of you. Why?" The fey began to circle around the clearing.

Songbird flew to Jaren's shoulder. If only she could make him understand why she had brought Ficiun here. *He is not your enemy,* she thought at him, wishing he could understand her.

Ficiun spread his hands and shrugged his shoulder, the bark of his skin creaking with the movement. "Why should I make her into something she is not?"

"You did it before, you didn't seem to have a problem doing it then." Jaren snapped. Songbird winced. This was going much, much worse than she had anticipated. Perhaps she shouldn't have harried Ficiun quite so much on their walk.

"Sooth, it is as you say. But now, the songbird has undergone her trial. The matter is concluded. The demon is dead. Her task, nay, *your* task, is complete."

"She wanted to do more, and you took that from her. We could have done more, together." Jaren tried to keep his voice level.

"He's right." Songbird chirped. "Please, Ficiun. It's what I want."

"Alas, there is naught I can do for you. The magic is done."

Why was Ficiun being so difficult? Was he just testing Jaren? She could feel Jaren shaking with rage. She tipped her head to his cheek, but he didn't notice.

"Why did you even come here? If you don't turn her back into a human, I will burn this forest to the ground, Brand's Bond, I swear it."

No! Songbird wanted to shout. *Jaren, I'm right here, we're so close.*

The fey narrowed his eyes which glinted dangerously. "Do *not* trifle with me, mortal. If you should try to burn down my forest, you shall be dealt with accordingly, in a manner both swift and cruel, for I will not suffer any threat to my woods. Songbird is a bird. She was always a bird, and she was always meant to return to being a bird upon the conclusion of her errand, though she did not know it. I say again, she has fulfilled her kismet and so returned to her true form. It is through no fault of my own that you assumed she would stay as she was. I do not bear the responsibility of your expectations."

"She wasn't finished. This isn't what she wanted." Jaren insisted stubbornly. "Change her back." His tone softened, "Please. I love her."

Songbird could see something in Ficiun's demeanor change. So he had been testing Jaren? Too anxious to sit on Jaren's shoulder she took wing. Ficiun moved closer, circling Jaren. Songbird hopped from branch to branch, trying to maintain the best vantage point.

"Mortals do fall in and out of love all the time. They take many lovers, and they love many things: power, money, jewels, beauty. Your kind love so easily and for such a short while. What guarantee would you give me that you will not discard her when she ceases to amuse you?"

"I will swear by all the Powers, the old and the new. I vow on my life, three times over."

"Such an impassioned plea, one may start to believe thou art indeed sincere in thine intentions."

Ficiun rubbed his chin with long fingers, considering. Songbird caught Ficiun's eye and bobbed her head up and down in excitement. "I told you he loved me."

"I am sincere. I would die for her." Jaren nearly snapped, his voice strained. Songbird had no idea his feelings ran quite so deep. He had confessed his love for her on the way home from Sauchvor, when she was in the basket. But he had not spoken to her of it since, keeping his feelings tucked safely away, as if they were too either painful or too precious to share again.

"Ah, but wouldst thou live for her? Therein lies the real question. And for her part, what assurance do I have that she desires to forsake her true form? Should her heart yearn to return to that of a woman,

how then will we know that it is to spend those days with you."

Songbird ruffled her feathers irritably. Now Ficiun was just tormenting Jaren, the fey knew very well what Songbird wanted. Jaren must have been equally as frustrated because he threw his hands up in the air.

"Ask her! If you don't believe me then ask her."

"Very well. If she denies you, what then?" Ficiun kept his eyes fixed upon Jaren. Songbird was nearly mad with frustration.

"Whatever answer she gives, I will accept."

"Sooth." Ficiun held his hand out again and Songbird glided over to it, landing on one the fey's long fingers.

"That was all rather uncalled for, I should think." She huffed at him. "I found you and asked you to change me back, is this sufficient proof that Jaren feels the same?"

Ficiun nodded, "Little morsel, I had to be sure. I will not give one of my own away so very easily. I treasure all who live in my domain, but I have grown especially fond of thee and I do not take this request lightly. I would not doom thou to misery if I could help it. Besides, it is far too easy to jibe at that mortal. In truth, I could not resist. But thou knowest, as the moons wax and wane, as the seasons change, so too do my powers. Autumn is for gathering, and winter is for resting, spring is for making. I cannot change thee until the spring."

Songbird's head dipped, "I had hoped. I will wait if I have to, but please don't make me wait too long. I'm worried I will forget."

"Thou wilt not forget, little bird. I promise." Ficiun said with surprising gentleness. He turned his attention back to Jaren, "So be it."

Songbird felt a wind, and the familiar tingle of sidhe magic. She could smell berries, wet leaves and the damp wood and winter rime. And then Ficiun was gone. She flapped frantically to keep from falling, as her perch had suddenly vanished.

"Wait, what does that mean? What did she say?" Jaren asked

the empty clearing. There was no reply. "Ficiun! What did she say!?" He shouted, his voice echoing through the giant trees. But Ficiun was no longer there. Songbird settled herself on a low branch, preening a feather.

Jaren came over to the branch, "What did you say?"

It was useless, but she told him anyway, singing her response as sweetly as she could, fanning her wings, trying to signify her encouragement. "We did it, we convinced him. Ficiun will change me back, we just have to wait till the spring. His magic doesn't work the same in the winter, but don't worry, I won't be going anywhere. I'll stay close so you won't miss me so much. I'll even sing to you if you like."

The first flakes of winter's snow began to fall. Jaren sighed, looking up at her. His black hair stirring in the breeze, dull now that the clouds had covered the sun. She could see uncertainty in his eyes, but also the smallest embers of hope.

Songbird by Iromonik

Thank you!

As always, **thank you** so much dear reader for spending time with my work.

Part of the beauty of writing stories is sharing them with readers. **If you enjoyed this tale, or any of my other tales, it would mean the world to me if you would leave me a review** on Amazon &/or Goodreads to help other readers like you discover my books.

I would love to connect with you online.

Find me on social media or sign up for my newsletter for the latest information as well as sneak peaks at upcoming books, artwork, and more.

- Tiffani_Sahara_Writes
- Tiffani Sahara Writes
- Tiffani Sahara
- Fliffani
- Tiffani Sahara

www.tiffani-sahara.com/newsletter-signup

More from the World of Galhadria

The Sellsword Saga by Dustin Ballard
Dueling Wizards
Mercenary Measures - coming soon

The Neversleep Scrolls by Phillip Walton
The Mind Thief Murders

Tales of Tigraen by Tiffani Sahara
A Songbird's Tale

Short Stories of Tigraen by Tiffani Sahara
Of Silver Wolves and Songbirds
Of Dwarves and Dragons

TTRPG Modules
The Temple of Grimbog
Dartak's Gambit

Music from Tigraen

You may or may not know this, but there is official music for the world of Galhadria! We've worked closely with singer and songwriter Arthur Rowan who is perhaps best known for his Star Shanties. He has written and recorded beautiful music for Galhadria, and it would be a shame not to share it. You can find this music on my website, the Blacksteel Press Website, or on my YouTube page. Scan the QR Code below to be taken to the playlist that features all the songs in A Songbird's Tale and in Dueling Wizards by Dustin Ballard.

You can find Arthur Rowan on Patreon and YouTube under Twin Suns Entertainment.

Sing the Dawn, Songbird's Song

The bird who lifts her voice at midnight lifts her voice alone,
Still waters aren't moved by the ripples of one stone,
So will this mean anything, in the end, when I'm gone,
Or is it still a foolish thing to try and sing the dawn.

Your farm girl stood the road, staff firm in her hand,
And faced down the demon, defending her land.
But did she achieve nothing but to choose where she'd fall?
And what if no morning light answers my call?

The bird who lifts her voice at midnight, lifts her voice alone,
Though I lay upon this altar all I am and all I've known
Will I have meant anything, in the end, when I'm gone?
Am I just one more foolish bird who tried to sing the dawn?"

But maybe all my choices, the great and the small,
Should better rest on who I am, not what might befall.
Though one single star could never brighten the night,
It can't help but shine. It's a vessel of light.

So though I lift my voice alone, I lift it yet for you,
To honor all you've given me, I must see this through.
Though I don't know what light, or hope my sacrifice will bring.
At heart, I am a songbird… And a songbird will always sing.

How Many Souls, A Song of Tigraen

Blood on the snow and a village aflame
And a horde turning southward to ravage the land
But there on the road stands a small lonely figure
Just a girl from the farm, her staff in her hand

Loud laughs the demon commanding the hellions
Tall stands the farm girl, determined and still
He speaks in a voice full of brimstone and thunder
"Tell me how many more of these fools must I kill?"

How many souls must fall to the fire?
How many souls must the dark overcome?
How many souls till Tigraen must fall?
Said the girl to the devil, "Every last one."

Though heavy the odds that are weighted against us
The last chance for victory long dead and gone
When others would quail and when all hope has failed
With the spirit of steel, we keep soldiering on.

How many souls must fall to the fire?
How many souls must the dark overcome?
How many souls till Tigraen must fall?
Said the girl to the devil, "Every last one."

So stand in the fire and sing in the shadows
Scream out defiance in the teeth of the storm
And should the day come when our nation is conquered
Damn sure there'll be none of us left here to mourn.

How many souls must fall to the fire?
How many souls must the dark overcome?
How many souls till Tigraen must fall?
Said the girl to the devil, "Every last one."

So, we shout to the devil, every last one!"

About the Author

Tiffani grew up on Lord of the Rings, Star Trek, and all-night video game marathons. She's a jack of all trades and sees no reason why she shouldn't have as many skills and adventures as her fictional characters. From obstacle races to art shows, she likes to do a little bit of everything. Like that time she ran away and joined the circus. Or that time she rappelled down a waterfall. Or that time she went ice climbing without an axe. Or that time... well... you get the idea.

Ever the dreamer Tiffani absolutely does not have a problem with taking on far more creative projects than any one person can reasonably complete, and she resents the implication. She lives in Colorado with her husband Nick and their two fluffy dogs.

Photo by Amy K. Wright Photography

Made in the USA
Columbia, SC
17 November 2024